A Fishy Color Story

JOANNE & DAVID WYLIE

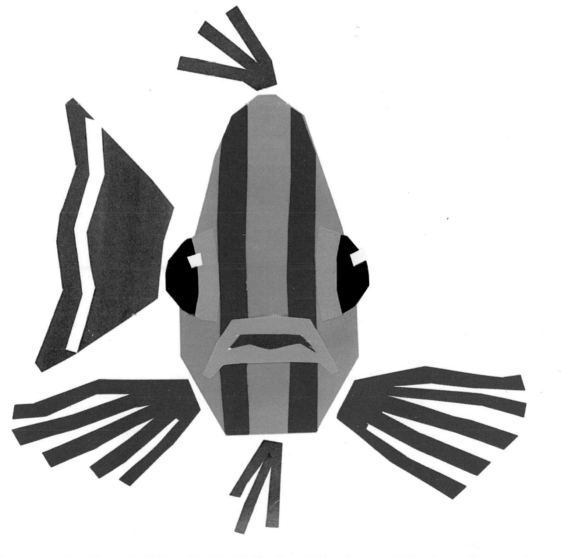

CHILDRENS PRESS Fishy Fish Stories®

JOANNE & DAVID WYLIE

A FISHY

Library of Congress Cataloging in Publication
Data

Wylie, Joanne.
  A fishy color story.

  Summary: A child introduces the colors while
answering questions about a beautiful fish.
  [1. Color—Fiction. 2. Fishes—Fiction]
I. Wylie, David (David Graham), ill. II. Title.
PZ7.W9775Fj 1983   [E]   83-7448
ISBN 0-516-02983-5   AACR2

COLOR STORY

This morning I caught a beautiful fish

but I didn't say what kind.

My friends asked, "Is it a red fish?"

I said, "Yes, but not all red."

"Is it a blue fish?"

I said, "Yes, but not all blue."

"Is it a green fish?"

I said, "Yes, but not all green."

"Is it a yellow fish?"

I said, "Yes, but not all yellow."

"Is it an orange fish?"

I said, "Yes, but not all orange."

"Is it a purple fish?"

I said, "Yes, but not all purple."

"Is it a brown fish?"

I said, "Yes, but not all brown."

"Is it a black fish?"

I said, "Yes, but not all black."

"Is it a white fish?"

I said, "Yes, but not all white."

It's a RAINBOW fish.

I wonder if it's good to eat.

All this fish talk makes me hungry.

WORD LIST (45 WORDS)

a	is
all	kind
an	makes
asked	me
beautiful	morning
black	my
blue	not
brown	orange
but	purple
caught	rainbow
color	red
didn't	said
eat	say
fish	story
fishy	talk
friends	this
good	to
green	what
hungry	white
I	wonder
if	yellow
it	yes
it's	

Joanne and David Wylie have collaborated on numerous workbooks, storybooks and learning materials for early childhood.

Joanne, born in Oak Park, Illinois, a graduate of Northwestern University, taught pre kindergarten, kindergarten and first grade for many years. She now devotes her time to writing materials that will help children learn to read and love to read.

David, born in Scotland, attended school in Chicago and studied art at the Art Institute and the F. B. Mizen Academy. He retired early from business and moved to the country to collaborate with his wife Joanne on a series of books for preschool and primary children.

The Fishy Fish Stories